Auntie Shawna,
Uncle Jon, Will & Zach

(Christmas '05)

Mrs. Goodhearth
and the Gargoyle

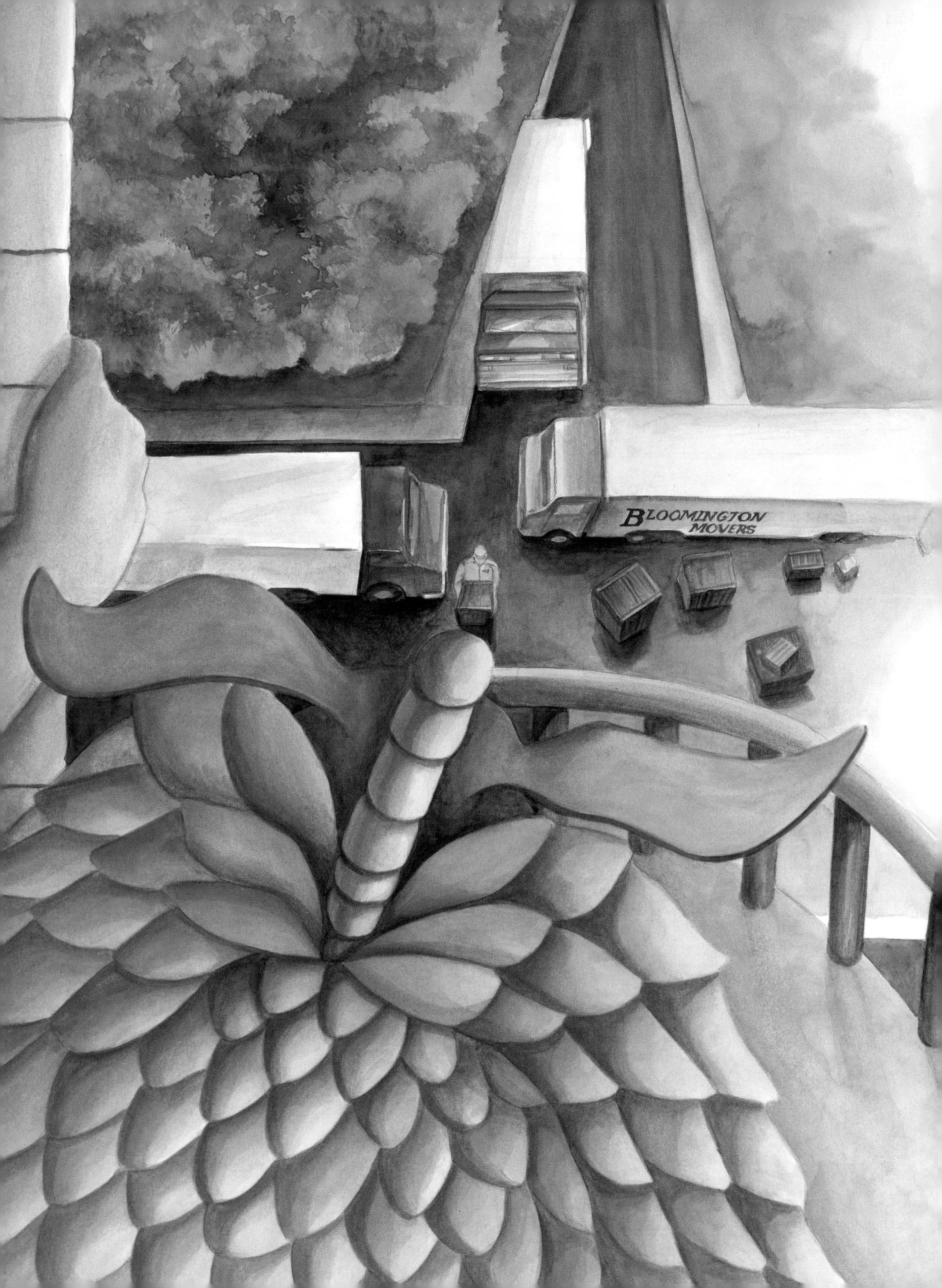
BLOOMINGTON
MOVERS

Mrs. Goodhearth
and the Gargoyle

story by Lena Coakley
illustrations by Wendy Bailey

ORCA BOOK PUBLISHERS

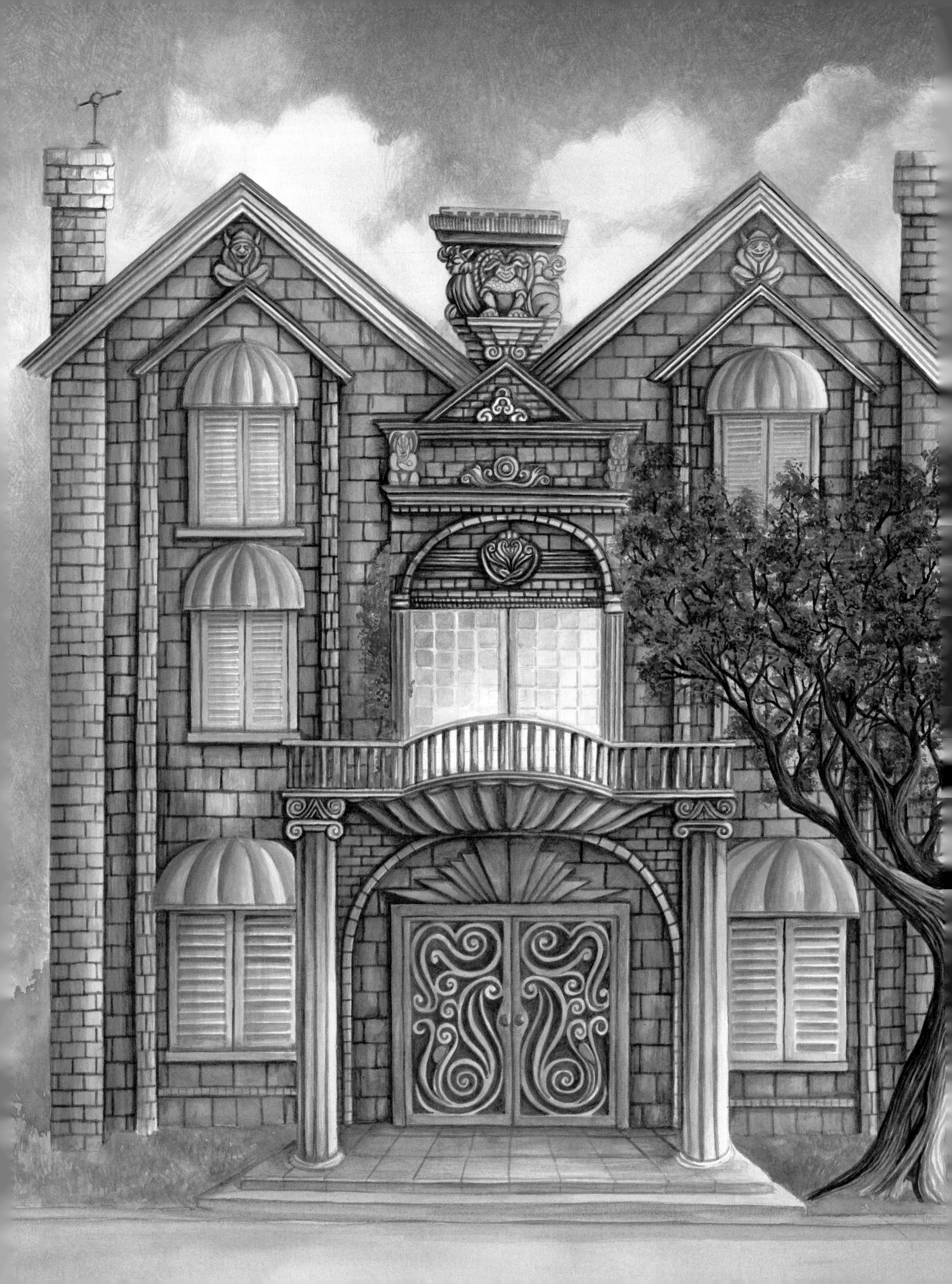

The gargoyles of Great House never moved—not in spring, when birds nested between their ears; not in winter, when icicles formed on their chins. They were all as still as stone—except for one.

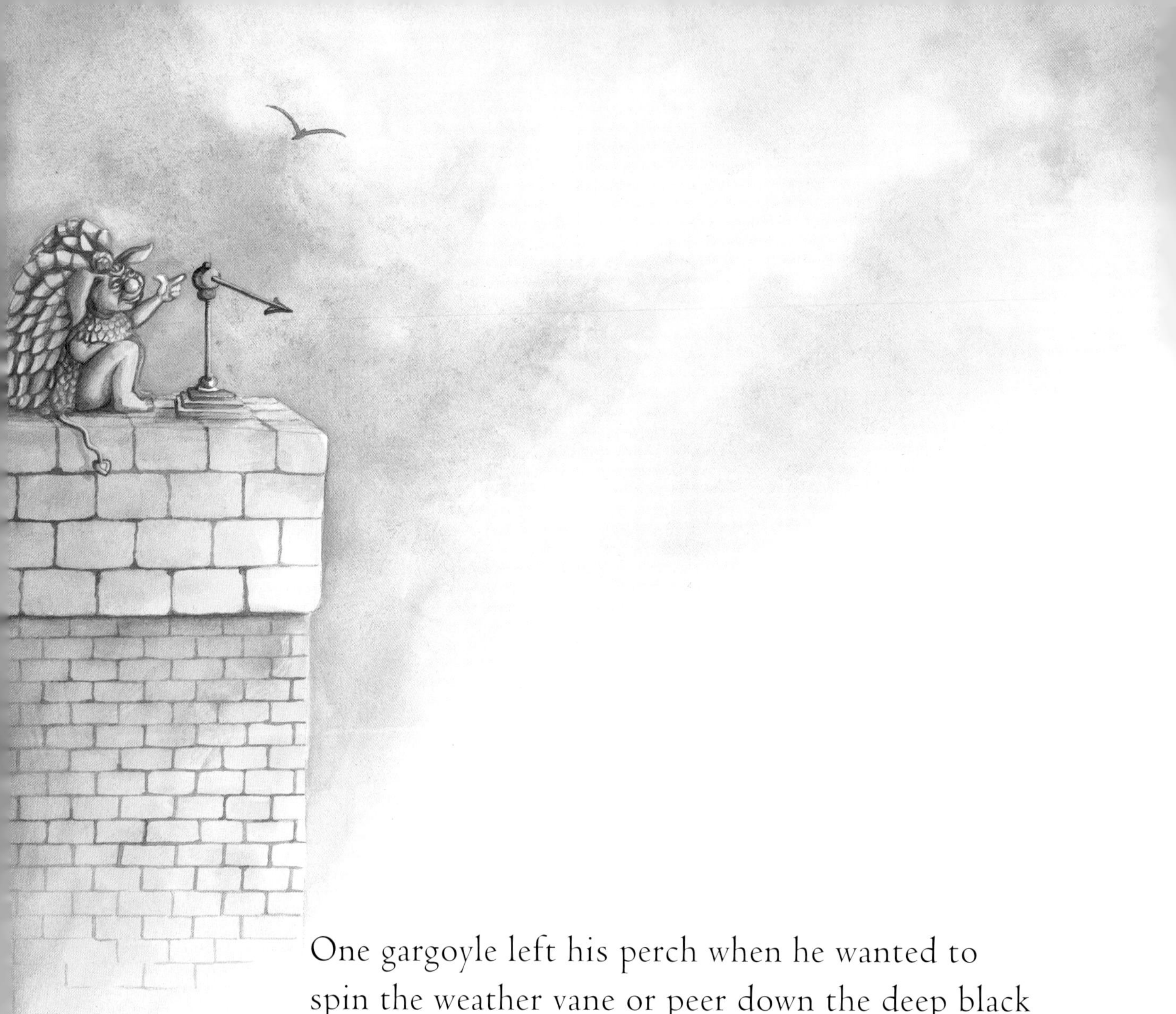

One gargoyle left his perch when he wanted to spin the weather vane or peer down the deep black chimneys. When it was cold he stuck out his long pointed tongue, waiting for snowflakes, and when it was sunny he sat at the very top of the roof, pretending that warm fingers were patting his scaly head. The Gargoyle often wished that the others would come too. But even when he poked them with his sharp little finger, they never did.

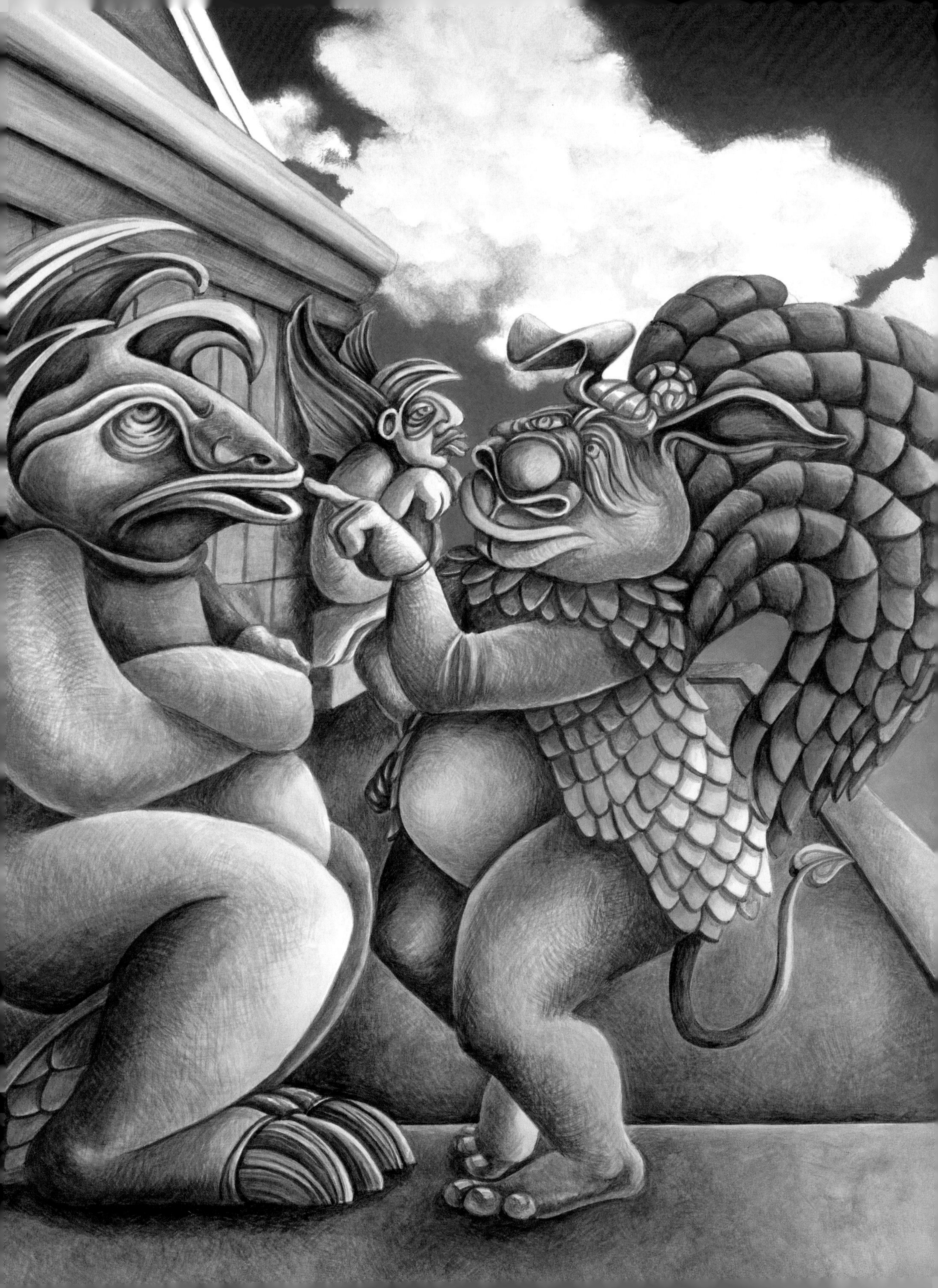

Then Mrs. Goodhearth came, with lots of exciting noises and trucks and boxes. The day after she moved in, the Gargoyle got a good look at her as she ate her breakfast on the upstairs balcony. He shook the crab-apple branches above her head until the blossoms fell down like snow, but Mrs. Goodhearth didn't notice.

He found an old acorn in the gutter and dropped it into her tea. Mrs. Goodhearth looked right, then left, then up. The Gargoyle wasn't in the right place, but he was sure if he stayed perfectly still she wouldn't be able to see him.

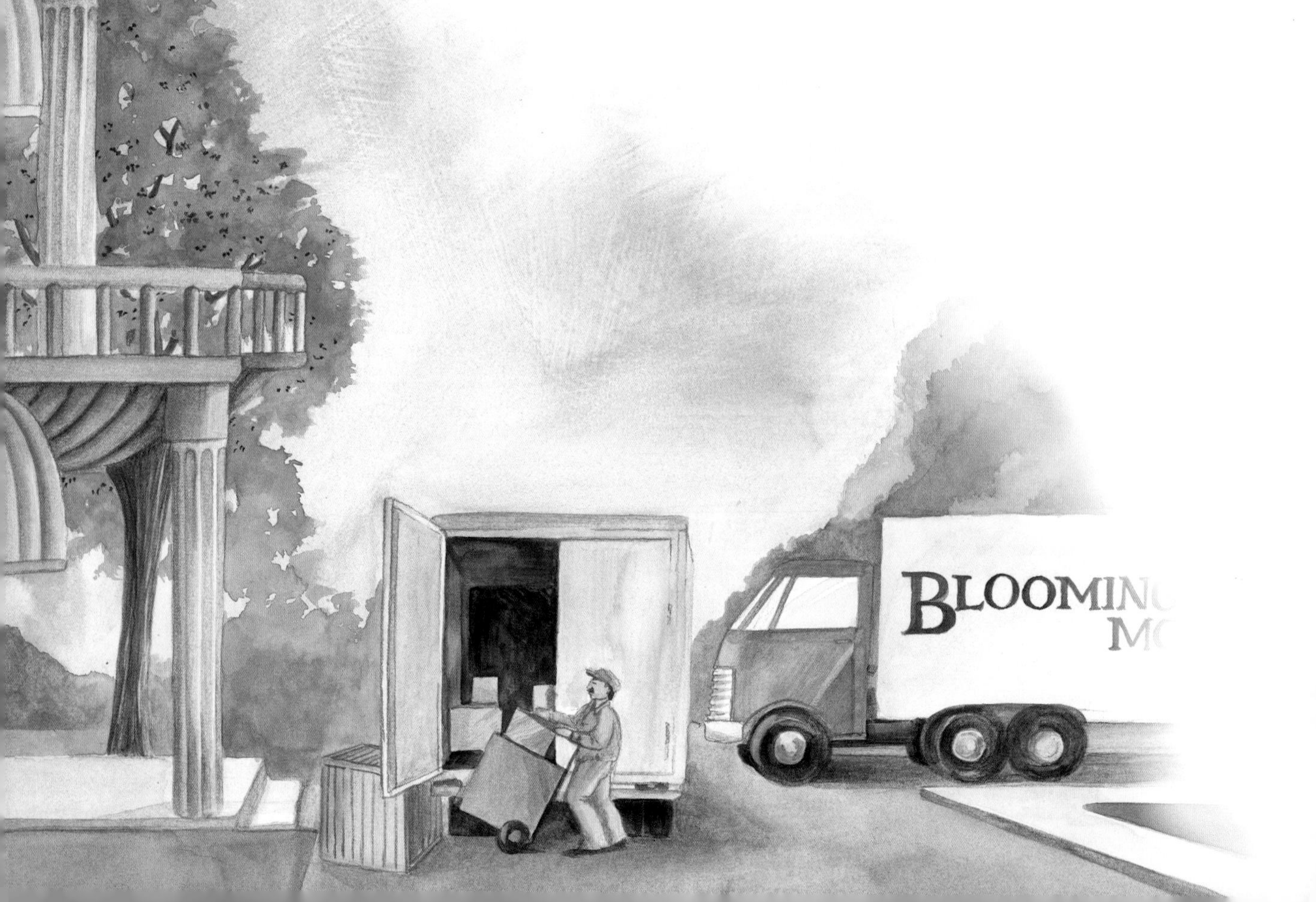
BLOOMIN
M

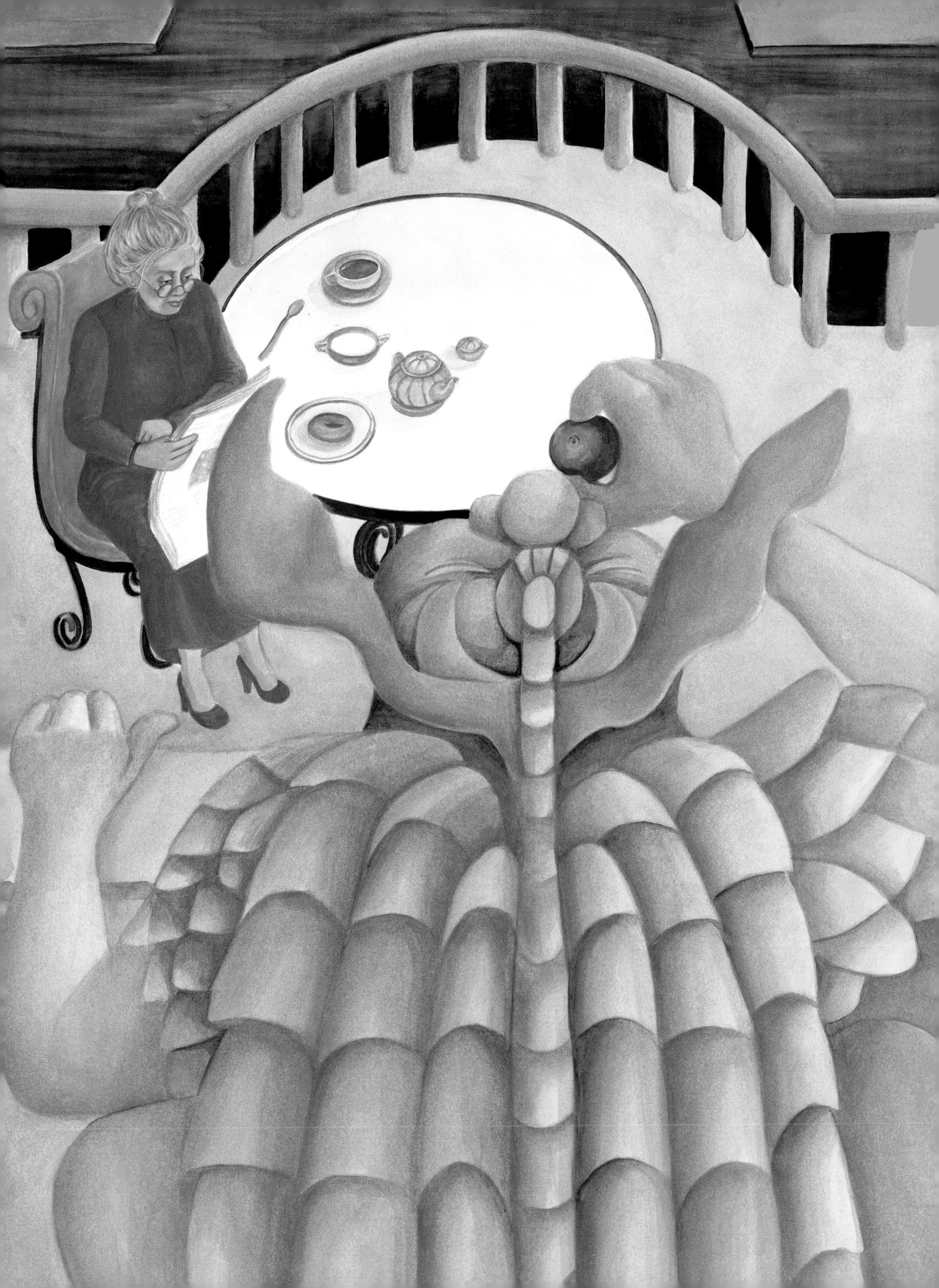

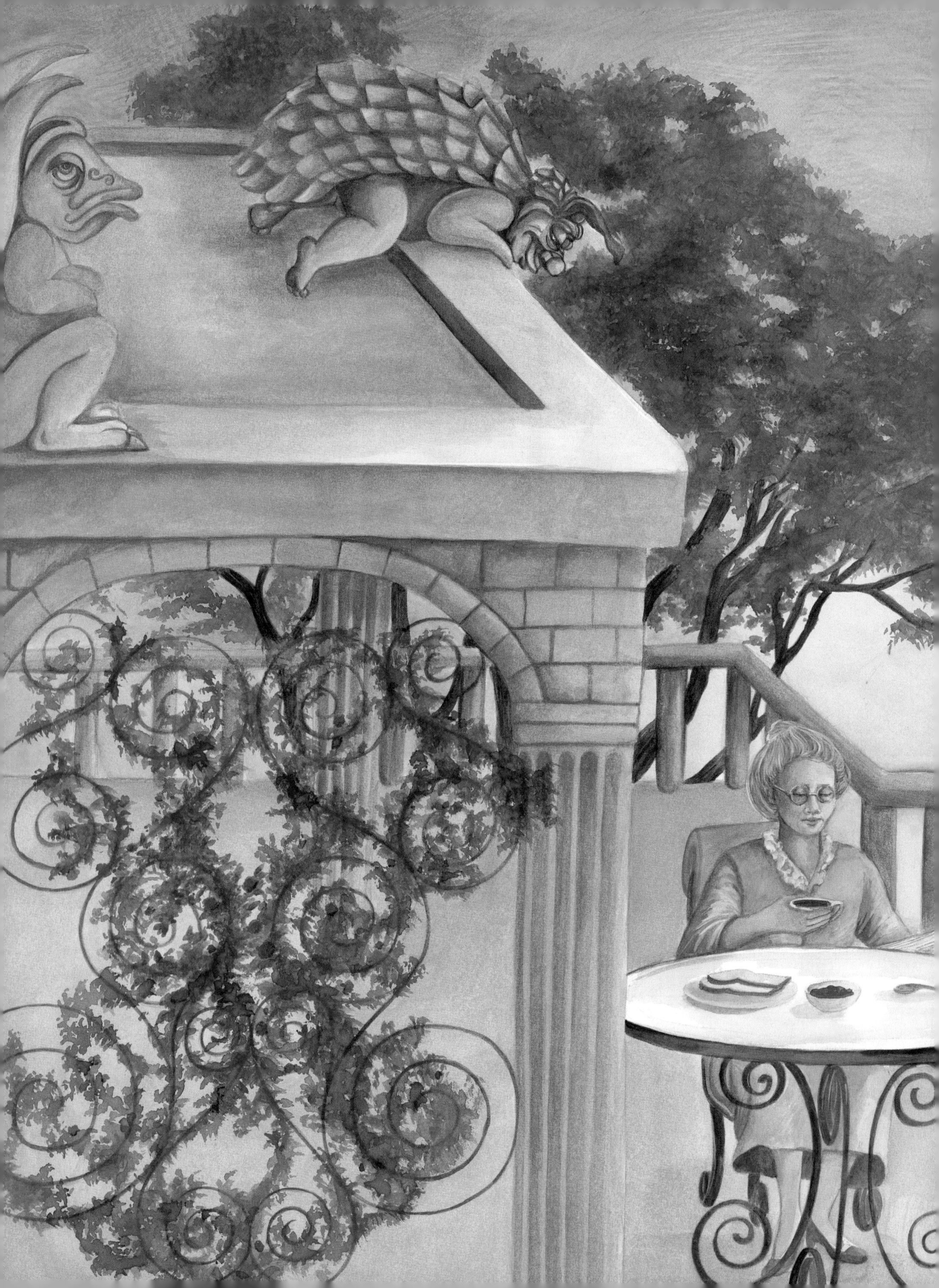

All that summer, Mrs. Goodhearth ate her breakfast on the balcony. Sometimes the Gargoyle spent a whole day looking for something good to drop on her. Usually it was a twig. "Oh my, what high winds we're having," Mrs. Goodhearth would say in a loud voice when it landed on the table.

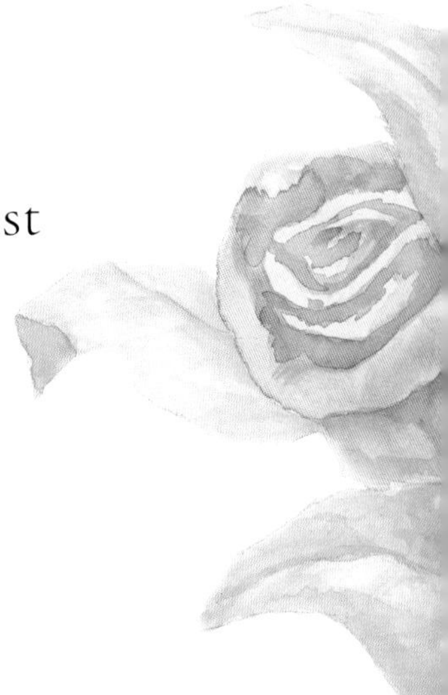

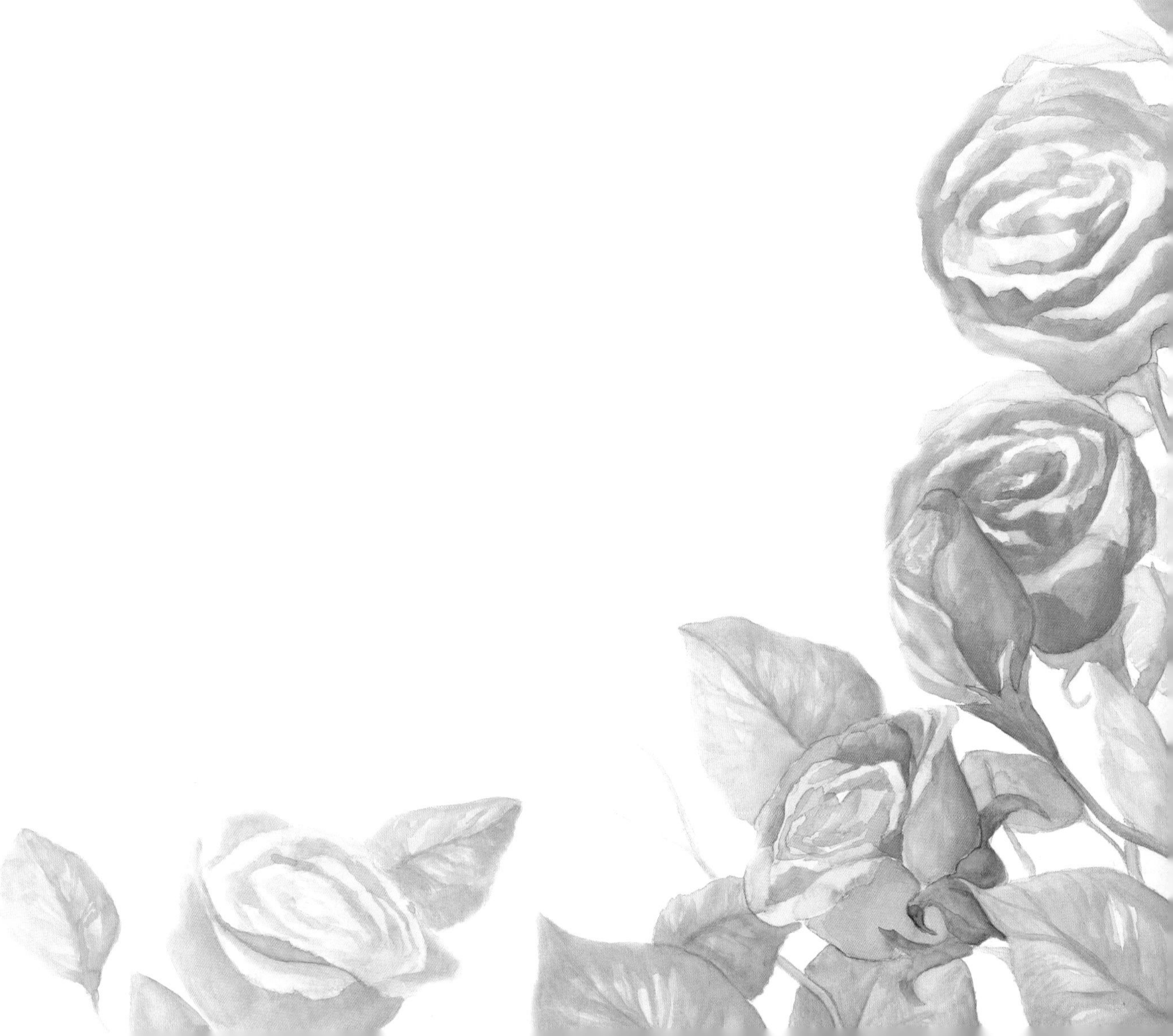

One day it rained. The Gargoyle waited and waited. The water ran down the creases in his face. It dripped off his bulbous nose. But Mrs. Goodhearth did not come out.

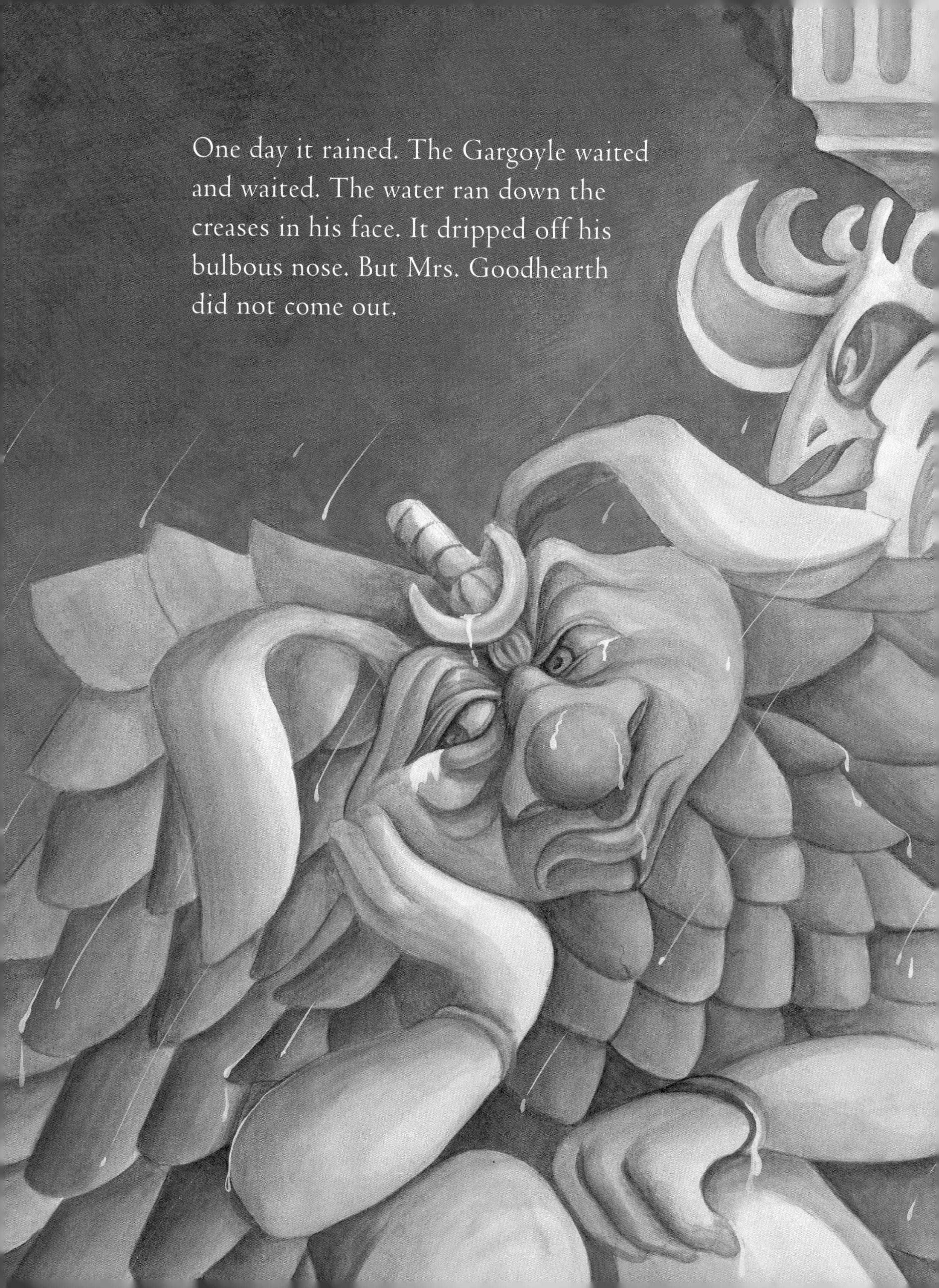

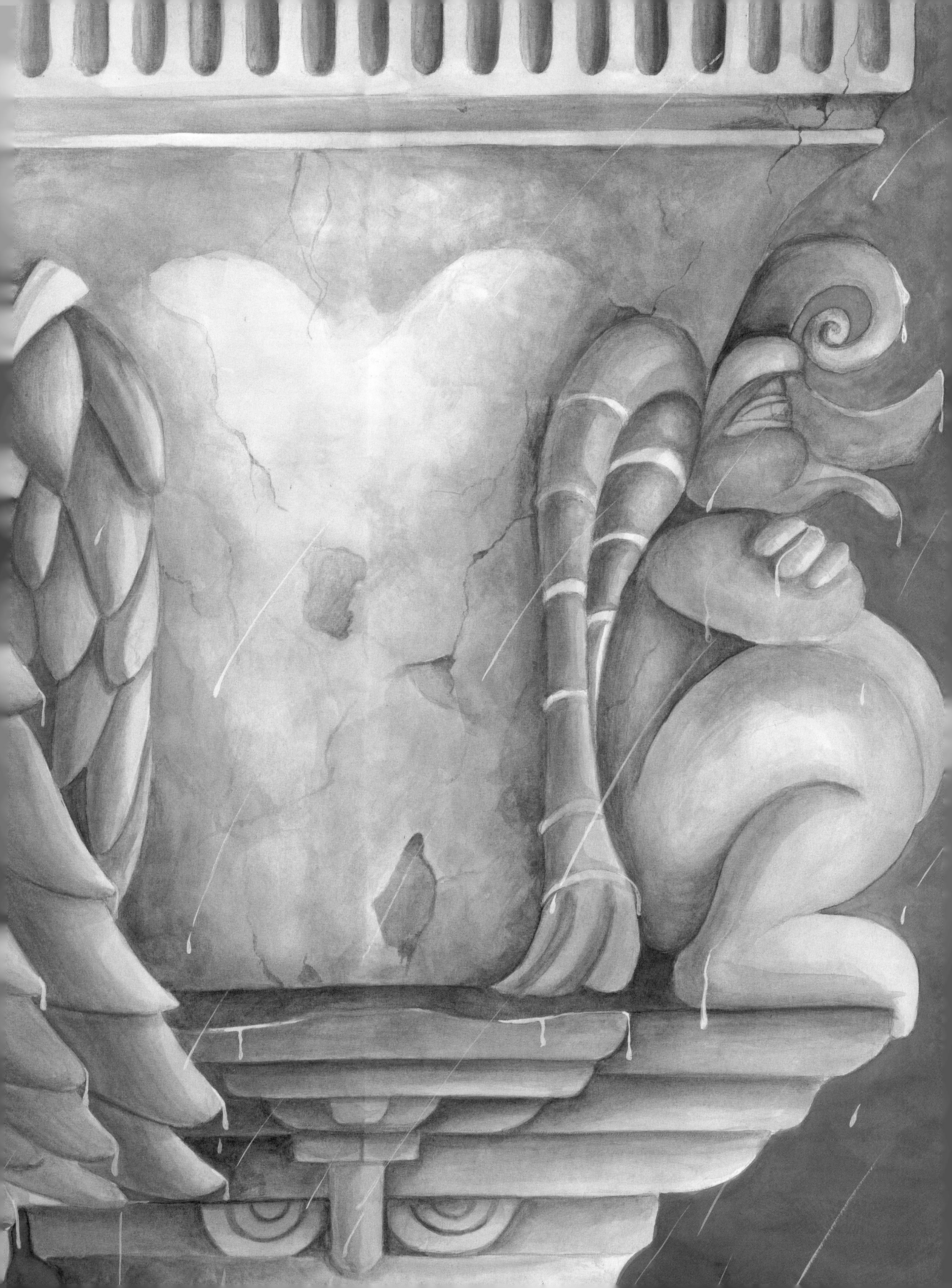

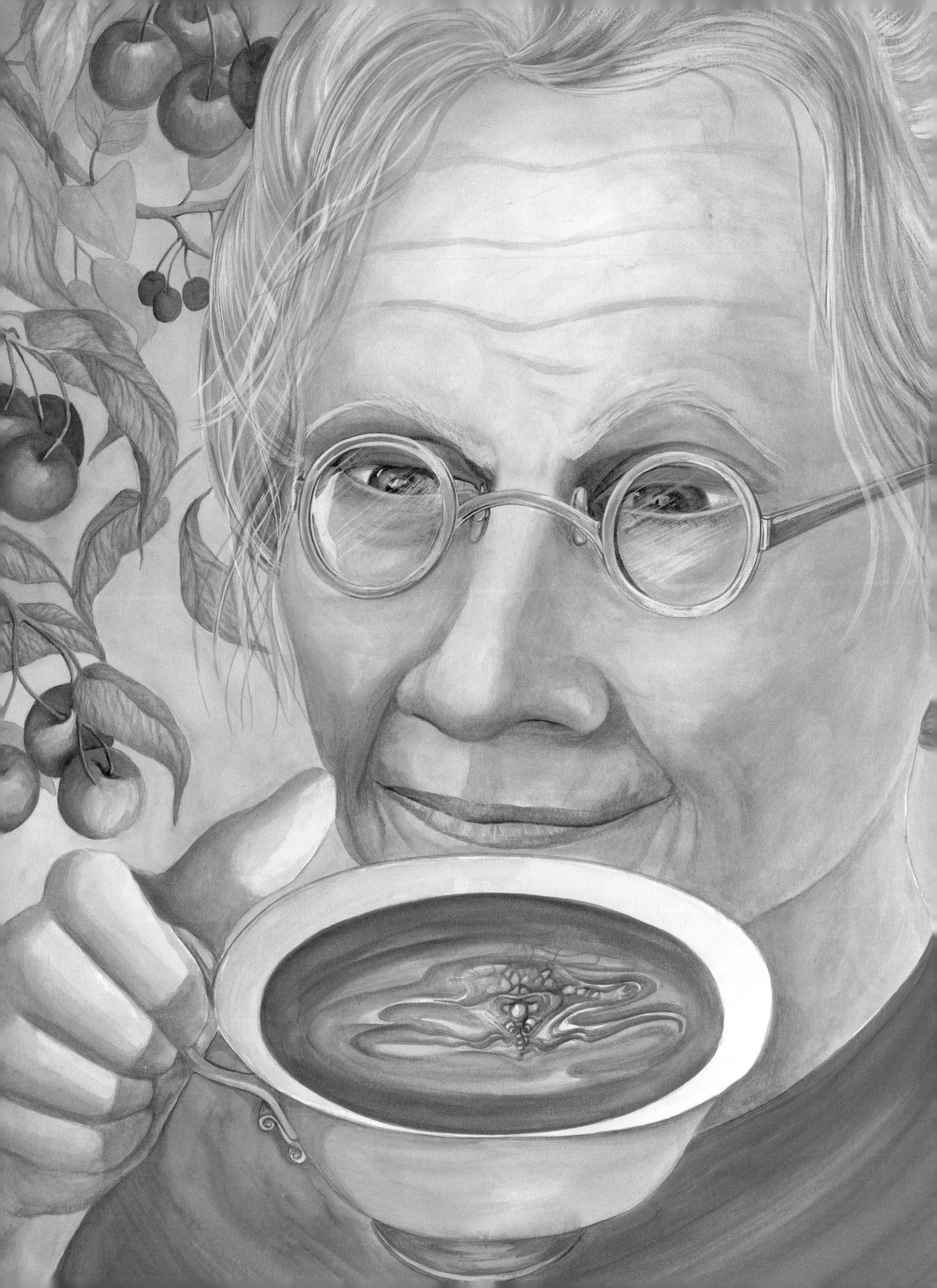

When it was sunny again, the Gargoyle flung hard little crab apples at Mrs. Goodhearth's breakfast. They bounced on the table and plunked into the cream pitcher. "Now these winds are too high," she said.

The Gargoyle saw the old lady's reflection looking at him. He froze where he was so that the reflection wouldn't see him.

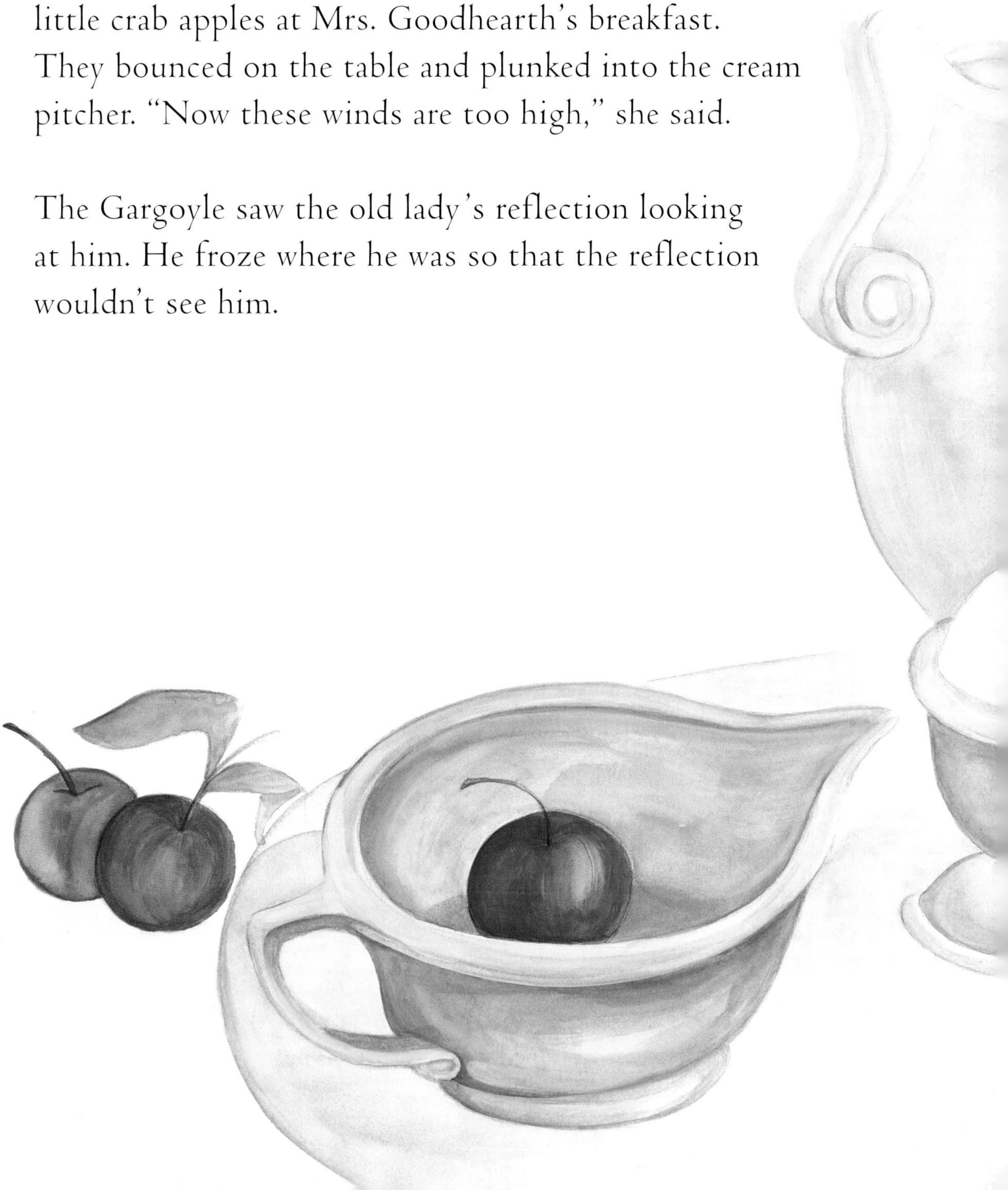

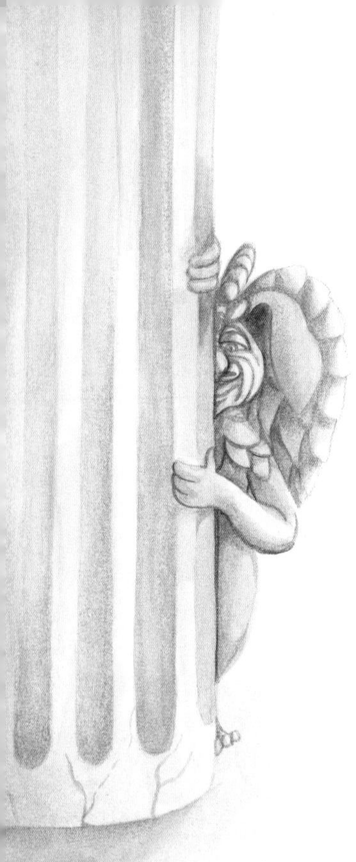

That day, Mrs. Goodhearth left something on the balcony ledge, something shiny and small. The Gargoyle looked at it for a long time before climbing down the rose trellis.

The balcony was flat, not slanted like the rooftops or thin like his ledge. It felt funny on his feet. At the far side were two French doors, but the Gargoyle didn't go near them. He grabbed the shiny thing, not even looking to see what he had until he was safe up high again.

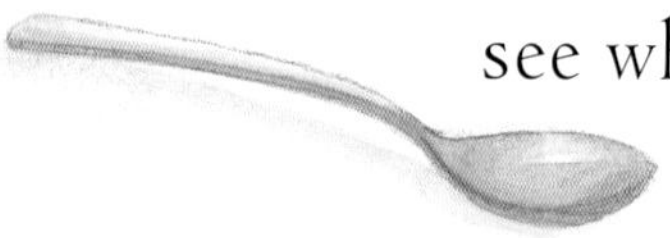

How exquisite it was. He wound his long tongue around and around it. He wove it in and out between his toes. It was a spoon.

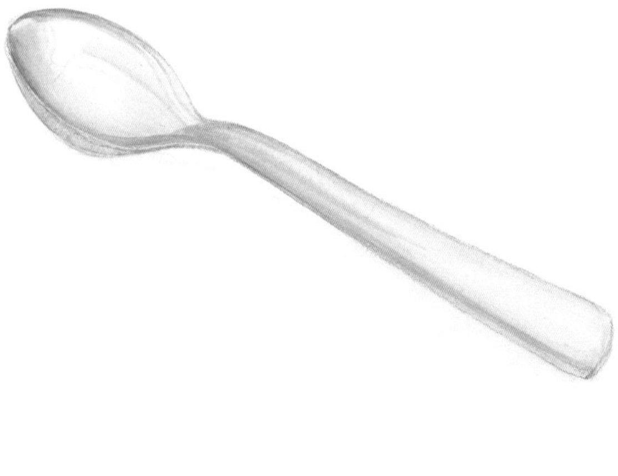

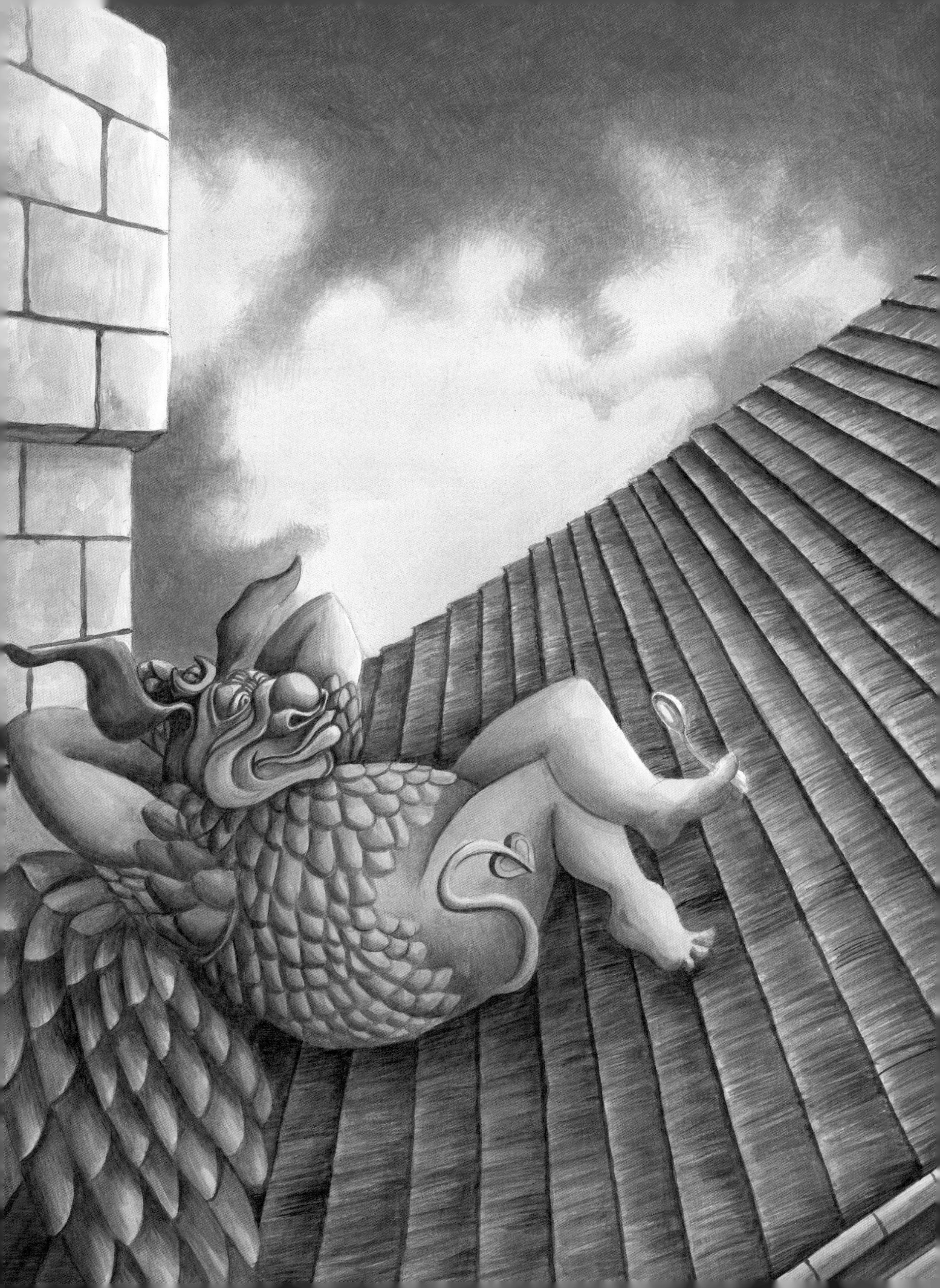

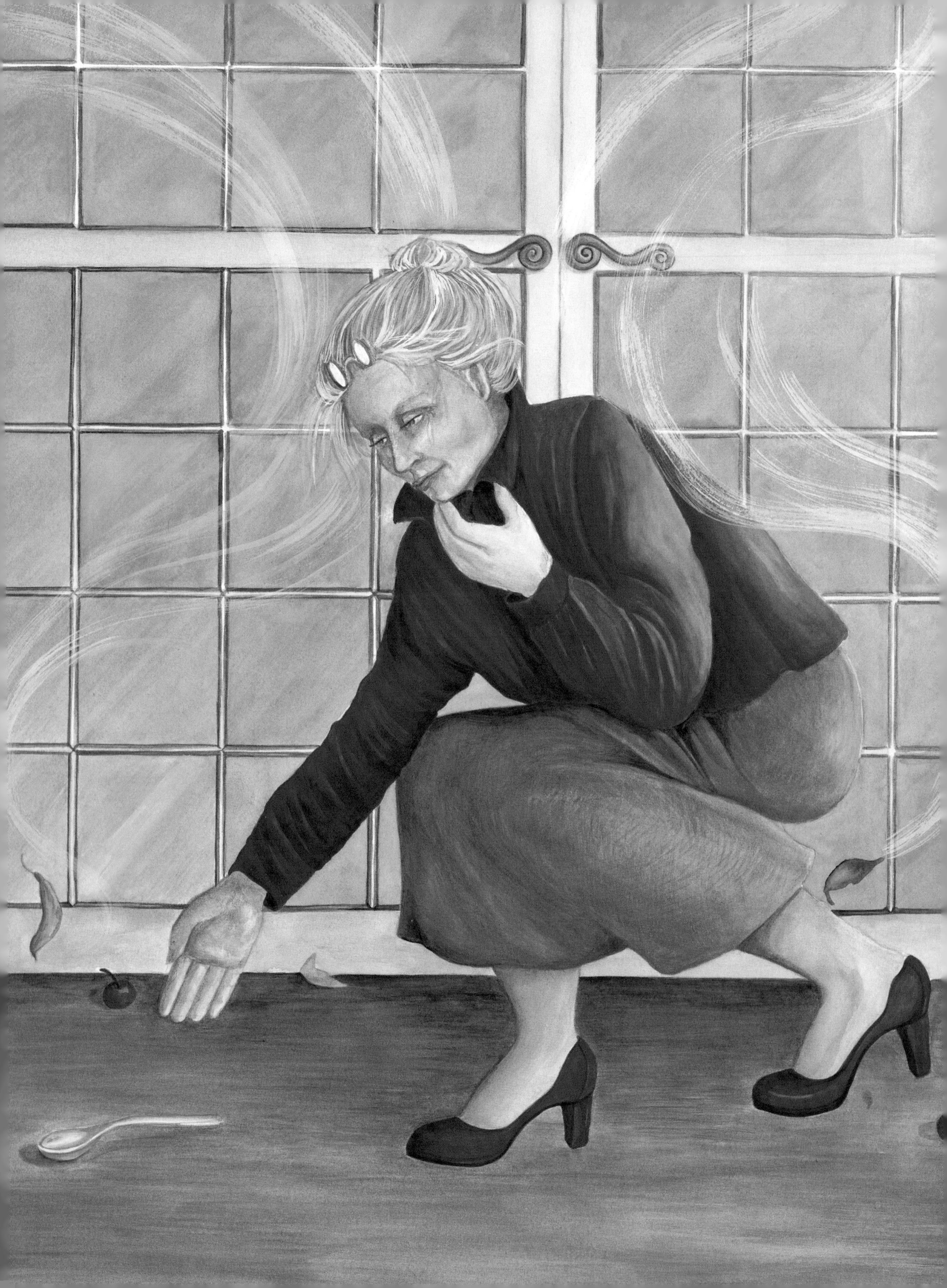

Autumn came. All around Great House the treetops turned from green to gold. Mrs. Goodhearth started wearing a sweater to breakfast. The Gargoyle didn't look for things to drop onto her anymore. He always dropped the spoon. And Mrs. Goodhearth always left it behind when she went inside. As time went on, she left the spoon farther and farther away from the rose trellis and closer and closer to the big French doors. Once, the Gargoyle put his face against the glass and peered inside. It looked warm and strange in there, but he didn't go in.

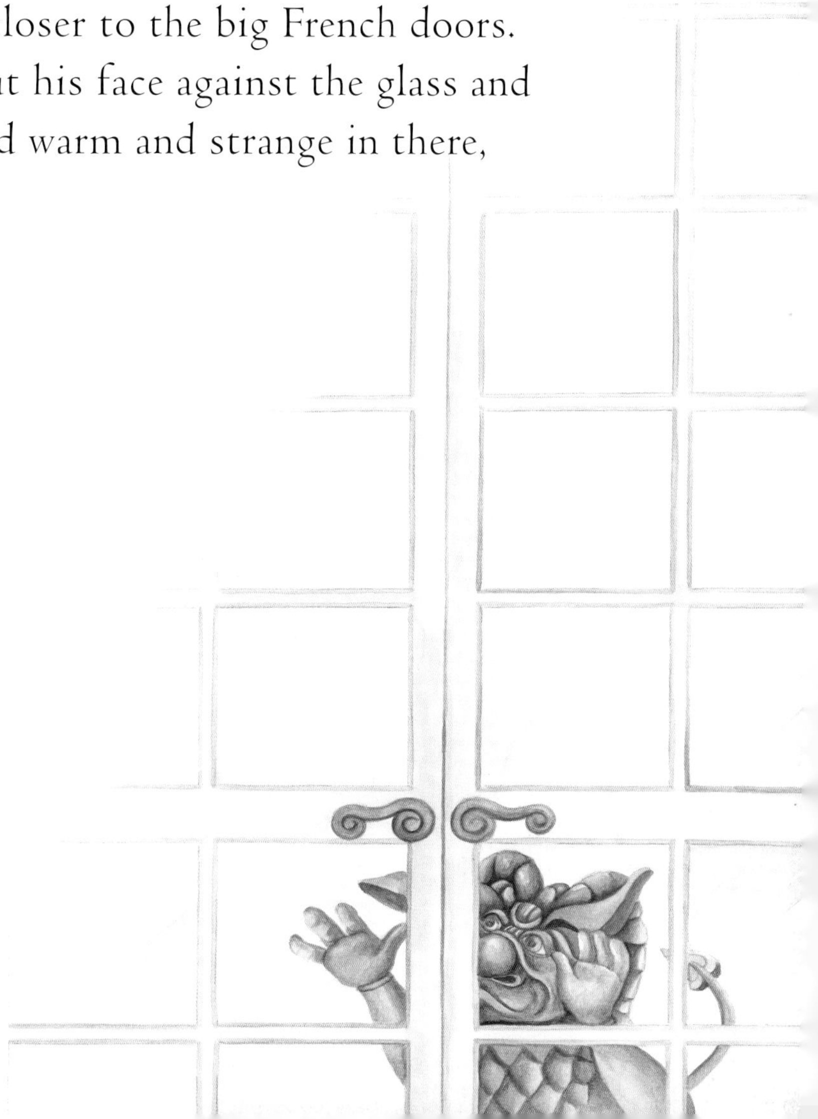

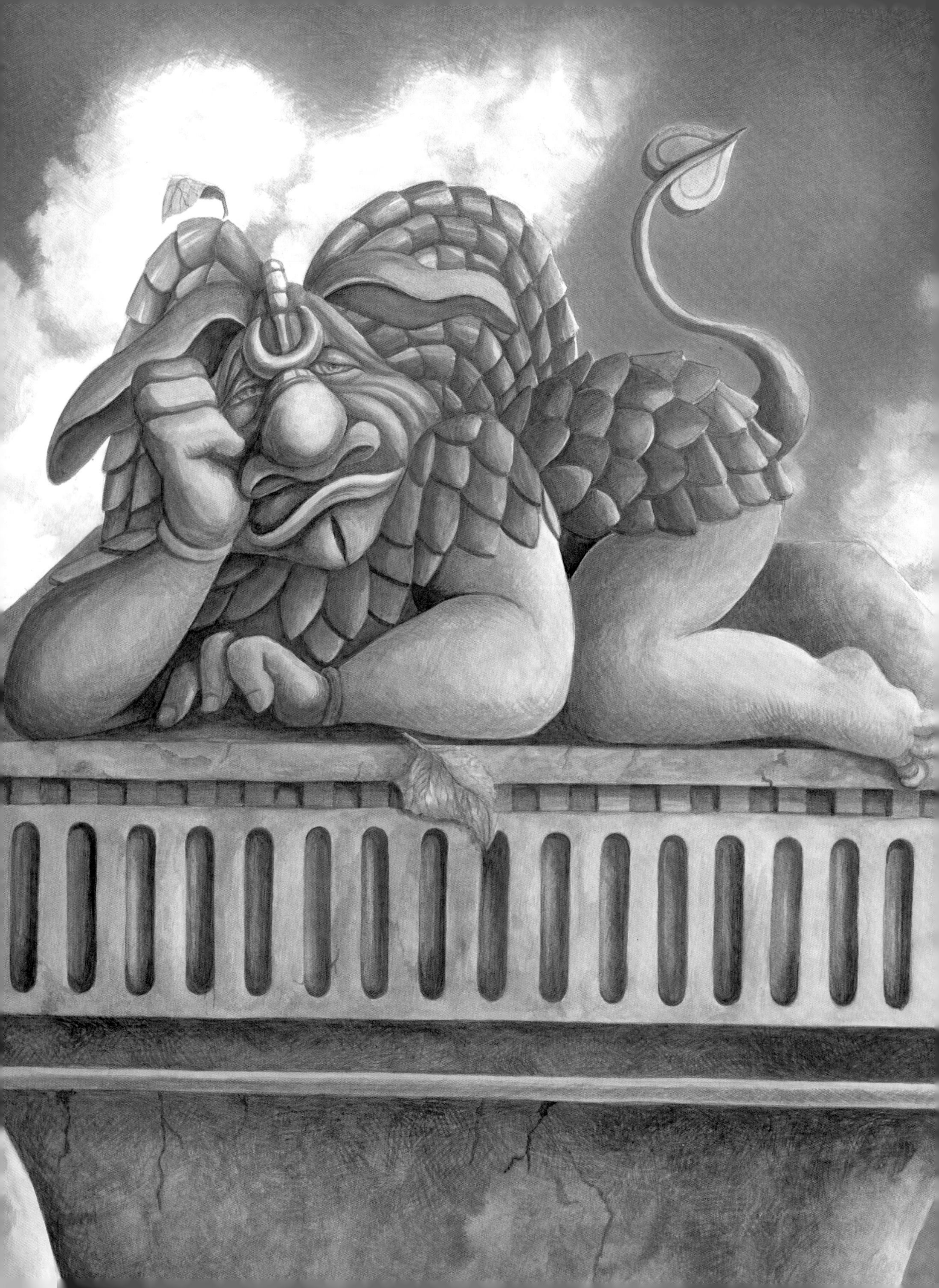

Then came the day that Mrs. Goodhearth didn't come out. It was breakfast time. It wasn't raining. Where was she? The Gargoyle clutched the edge of the roof with his toes, waiting. The sun arced over his head and disappeared into the leafless branches.

The next day, he waited again.

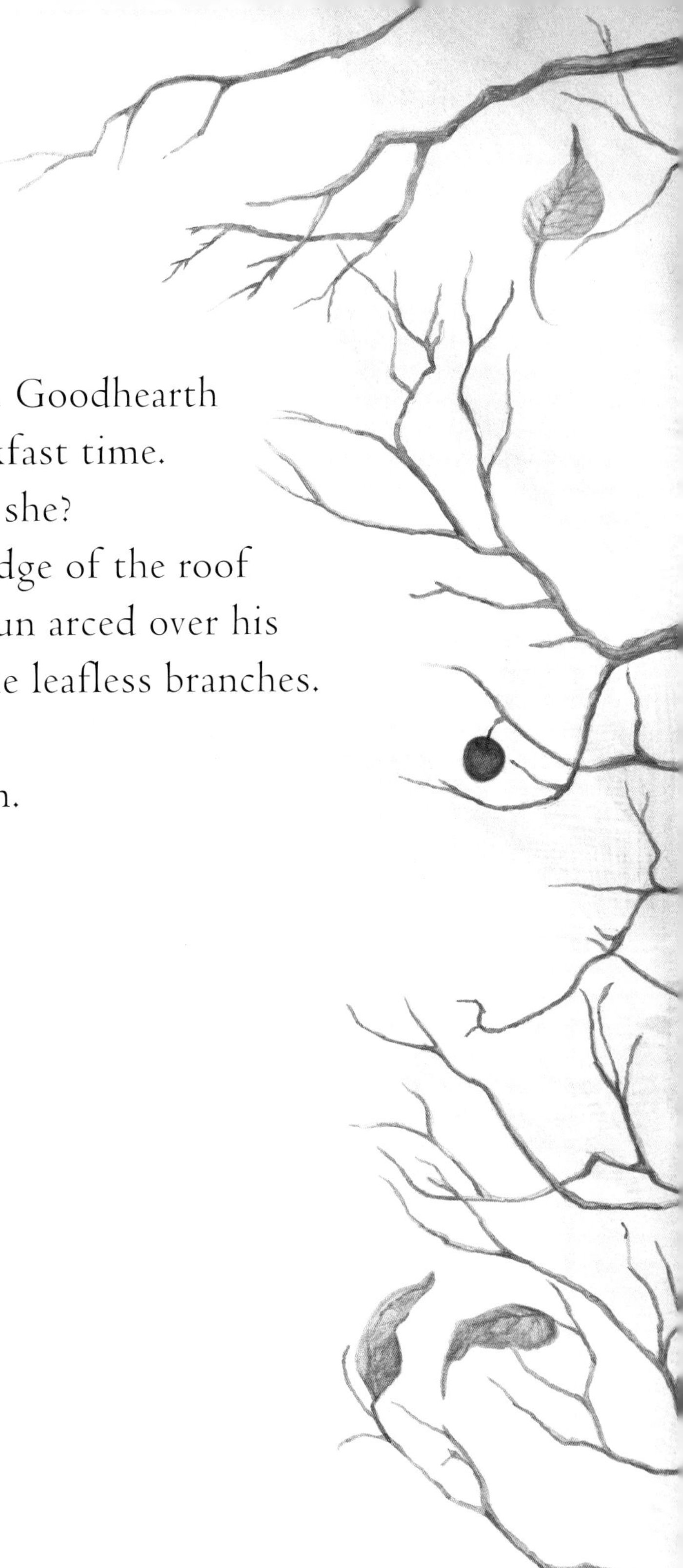

On the third day, it began to snow. It reminded the Gargoyle of the time he had shaken the apple blossoms onto Mrs. Goodhearth's head so long ago. The wind gusted around the chimneys, making a forlorn sound. She had forgotten him.

The Gargoyle threw his spoon at the deserted breakfast table. It bounced off the balcony ledge and clattered all the way down to the low, low ground. Gone. The Gargoyle went back to his ledge and sat in his place between the others. He would be like them now, he decided. He would let the birds nest between his ears and the icicles form on his chin. He would be as still as sadness.

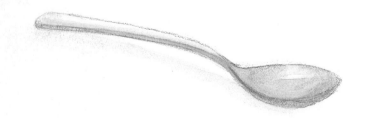

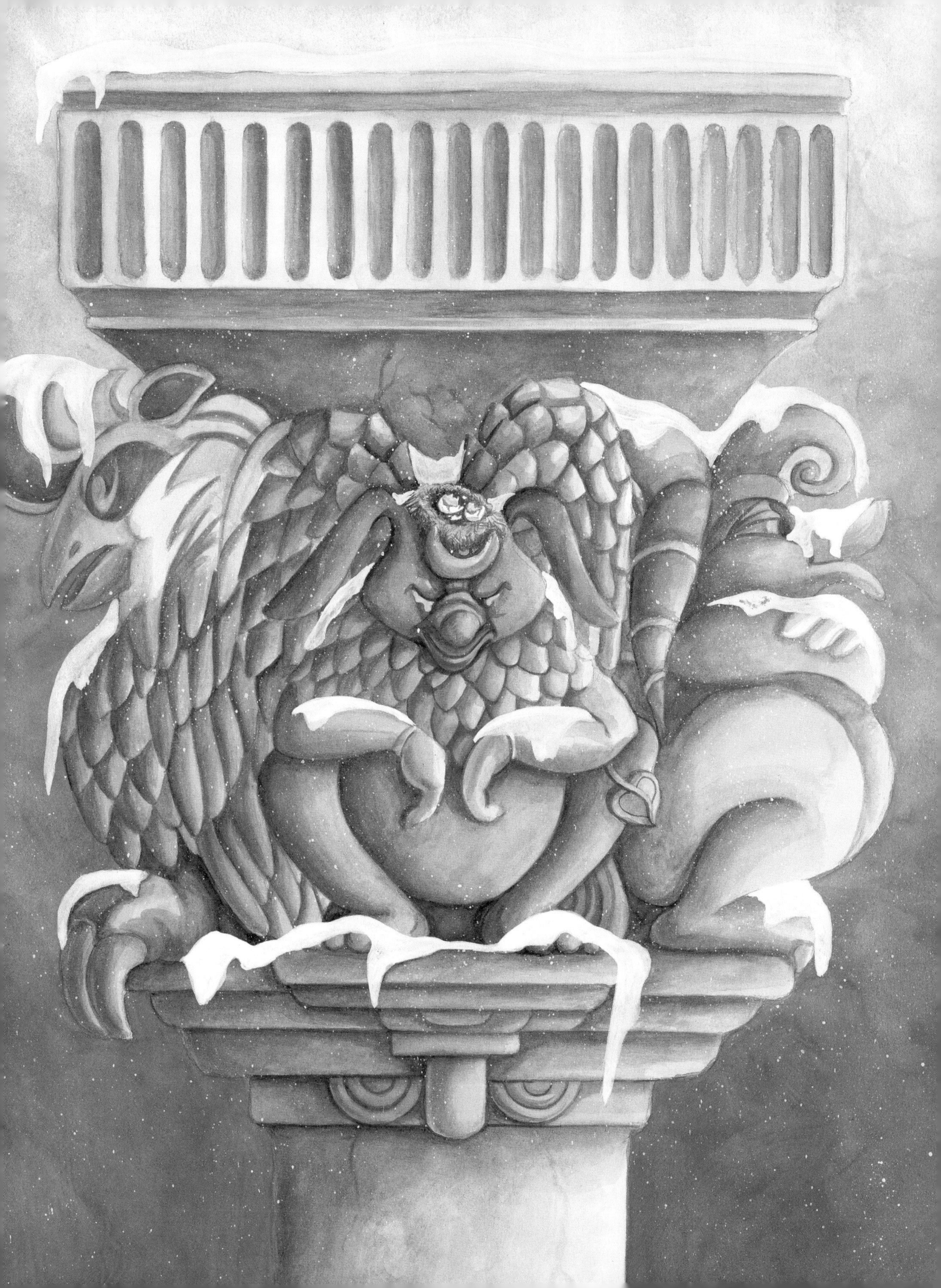

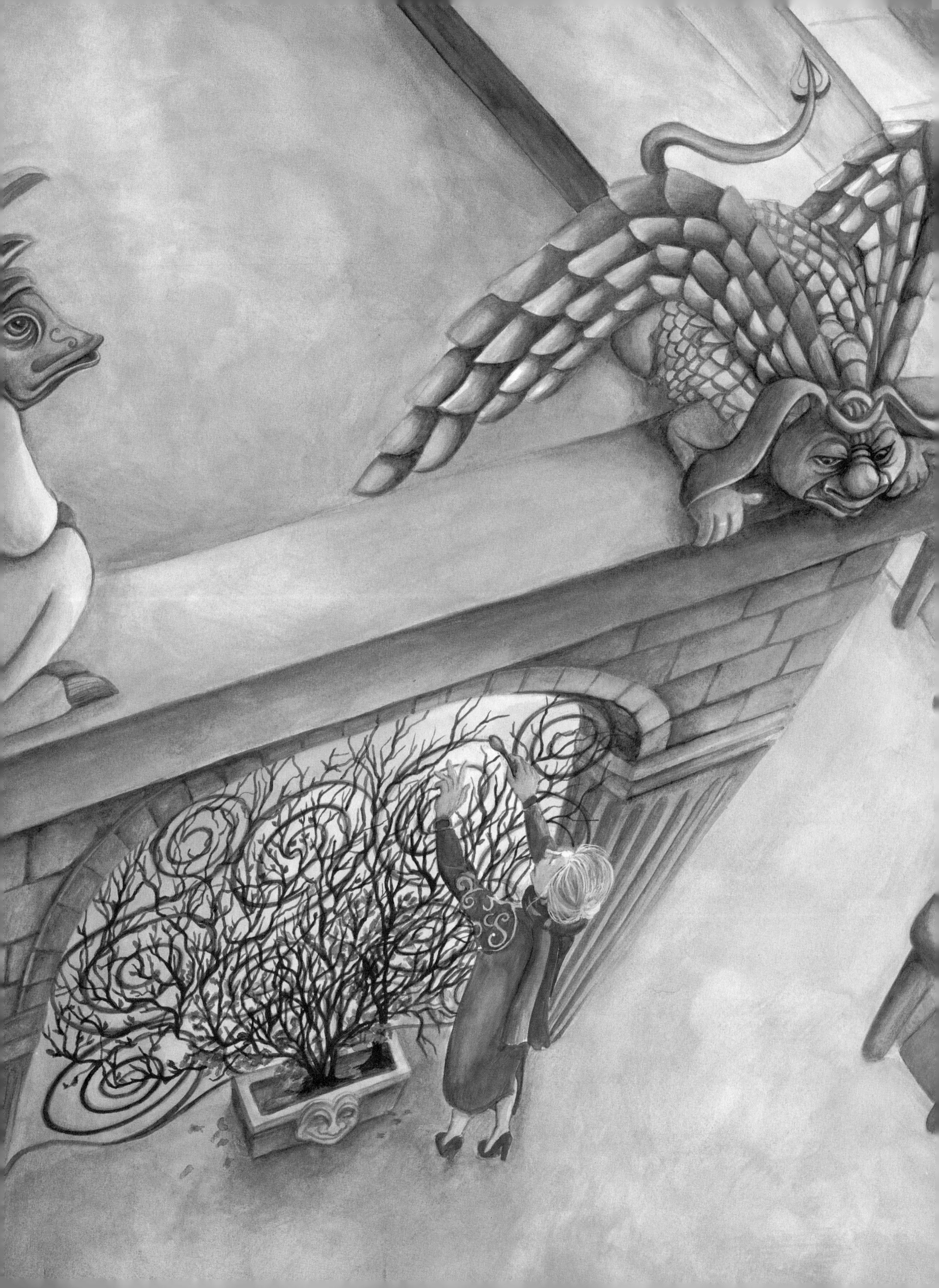

Something hit him on the foot. Then something else hit his knee. Down below, Mrs. Goodhearth was throwing sticks at him. She wore a fluffy, red scarf, and her white breath rose up to him like puffs of chimney smoke. He stayed very still, but even so, he had a feeling that she could see him. After a while, Mrs. Goodhearth held up a spoon. She stood on tiptoe and wove it into the dry vines of the trellis. When she went inside, the Gargoyle rushed to get it. Oh, his dear spoon. He had thought he'd never see it again. But from the trellis, he noticed another spoon on the balcony ledge. And two others by the table and the French doors. He followed the trail.

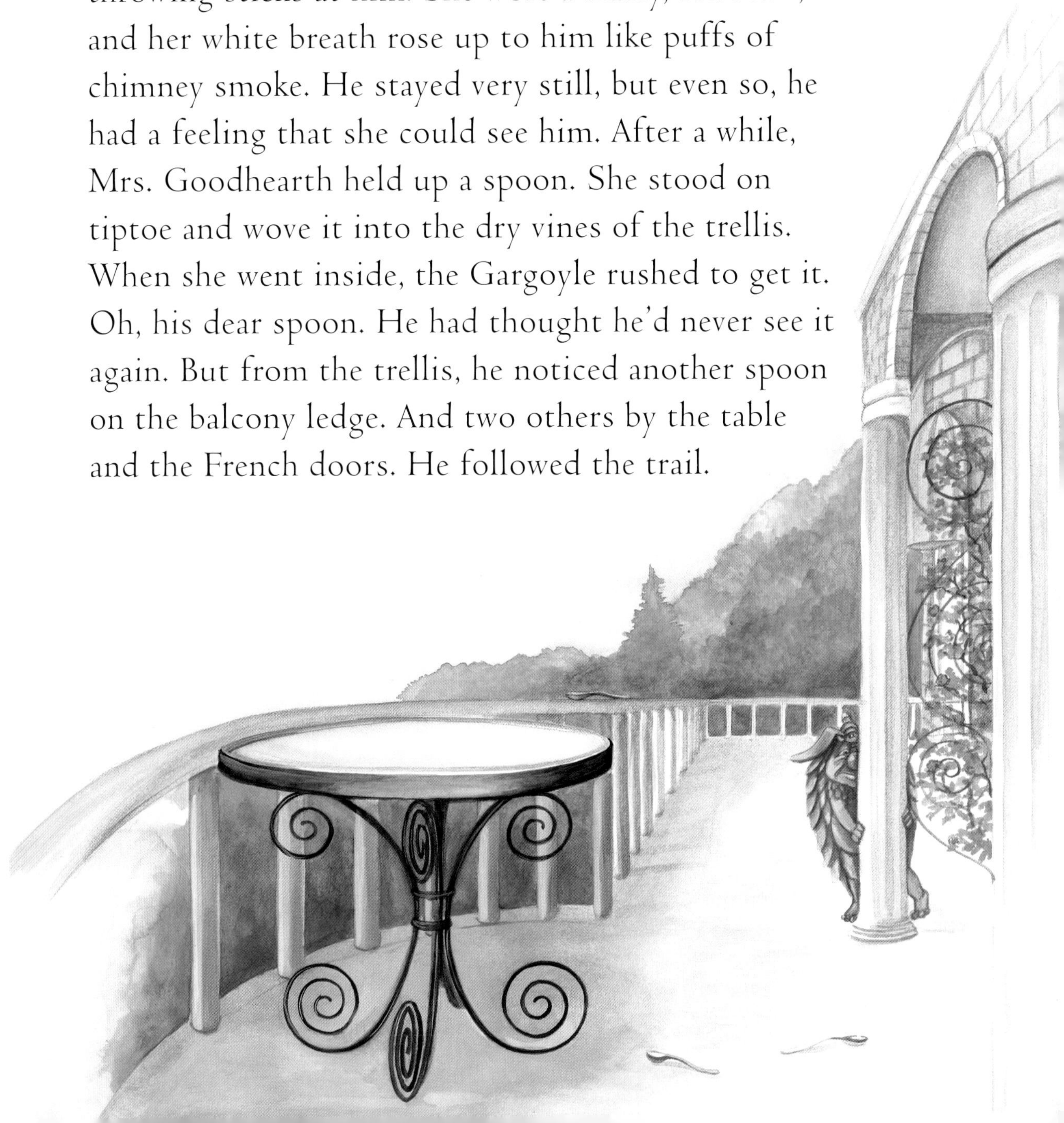

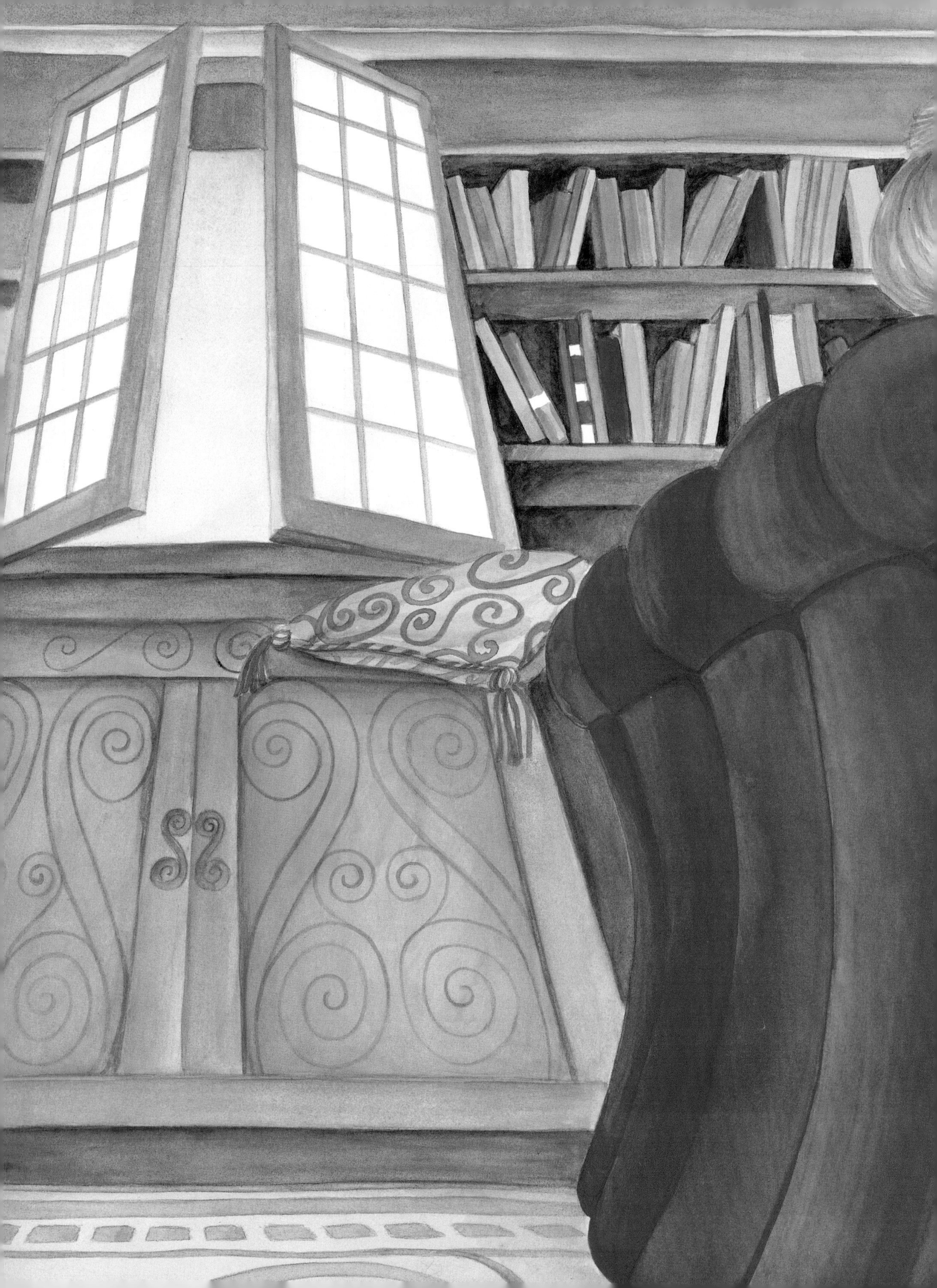

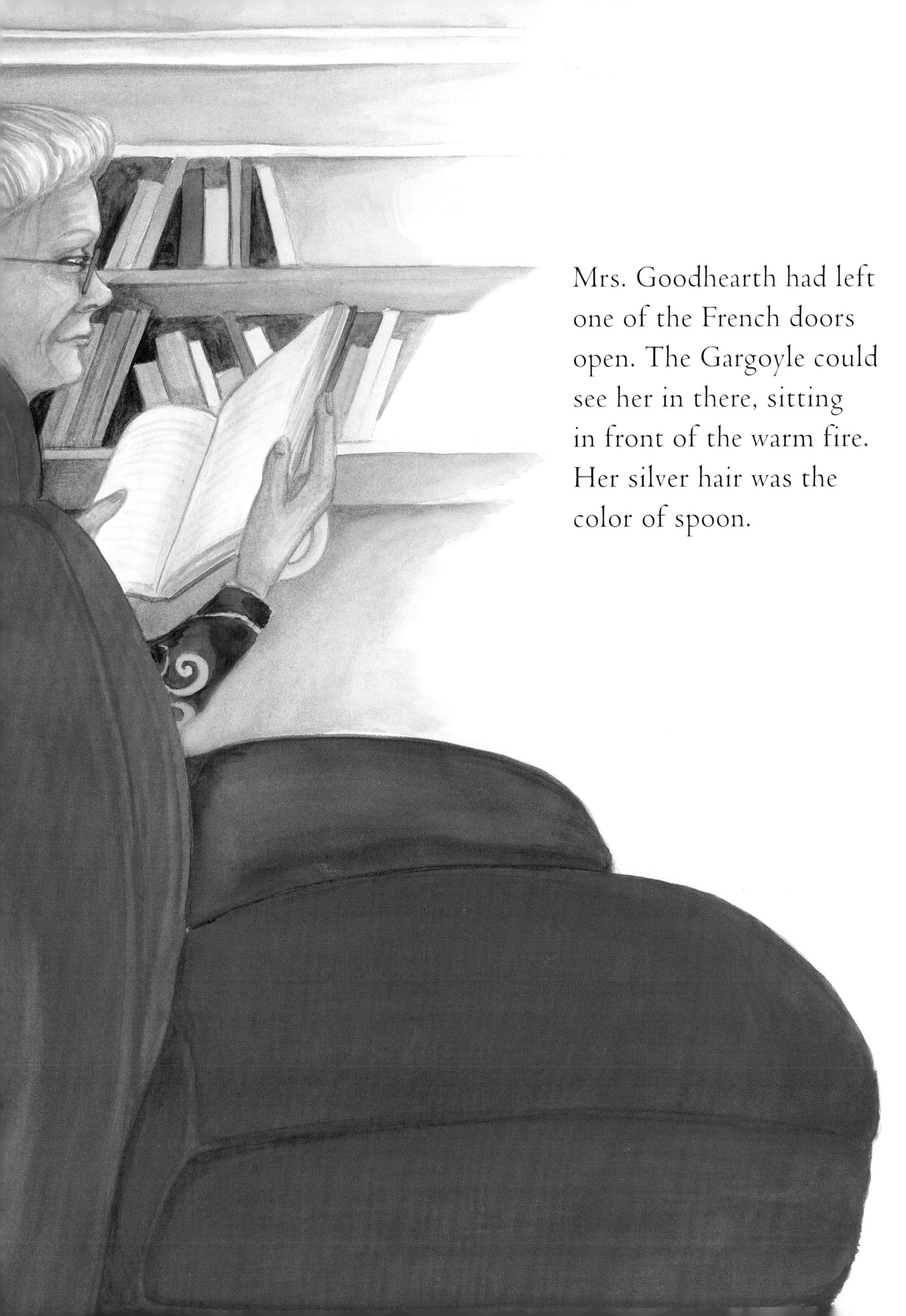

Mrs. Goodhearth had left one of the French doors open. The Gargoyle could see her in there, sitting in front of the warm fire. Her silver hair was the color of spoon.

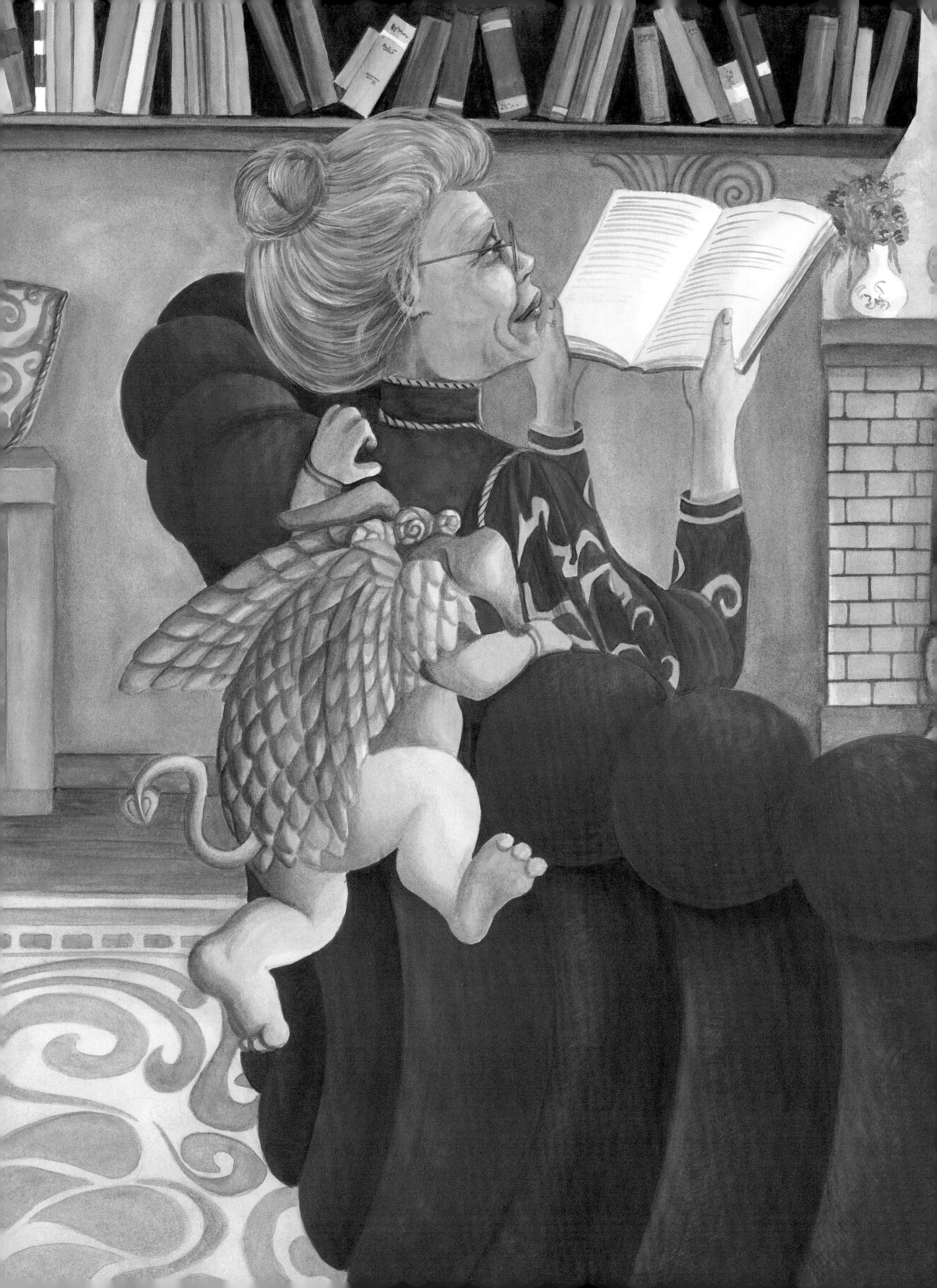

Inside was strange. The sky was very pale and close.
The Gargoyle's toes made a clicking sound on the
floor. Slowly he crept up behind Mrs. Goodhearth.
"My, what a good book I'm reading," she said loudly.
The Gargoyle climbed up the back of the couch to
perch behind her. Mrs. Goodhearth looked more like
herself, now that he could look down at the top of her
head. The Gargoyle took a single strand of the old
lady's hair between his fingers and plucked.

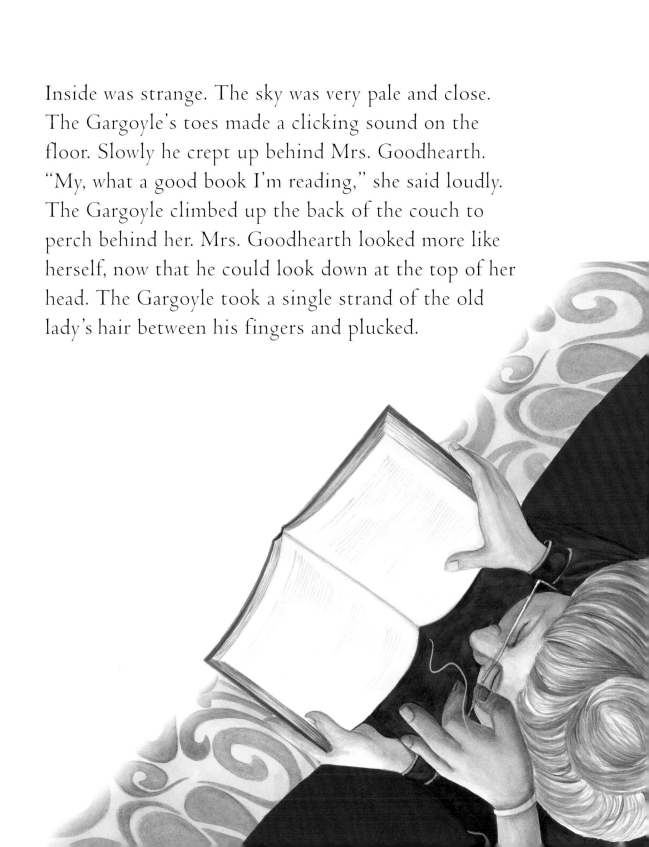

"No, no, no, dear," said Mrs. Goodhearth. She turned and put her hand gently on the Gargoyle's knobby knee.

The Gargoyle smiled. He didn't try to stay still so that she wouldn't see him. Instead, he leaned down until his head was resting on Mrs. Goodhearth's shoulder. He handed her what he had collected—a bouquet of spoons.

"Lovely," she said. She stroked him between the ears. And her fingers felt as warm as sunshine.

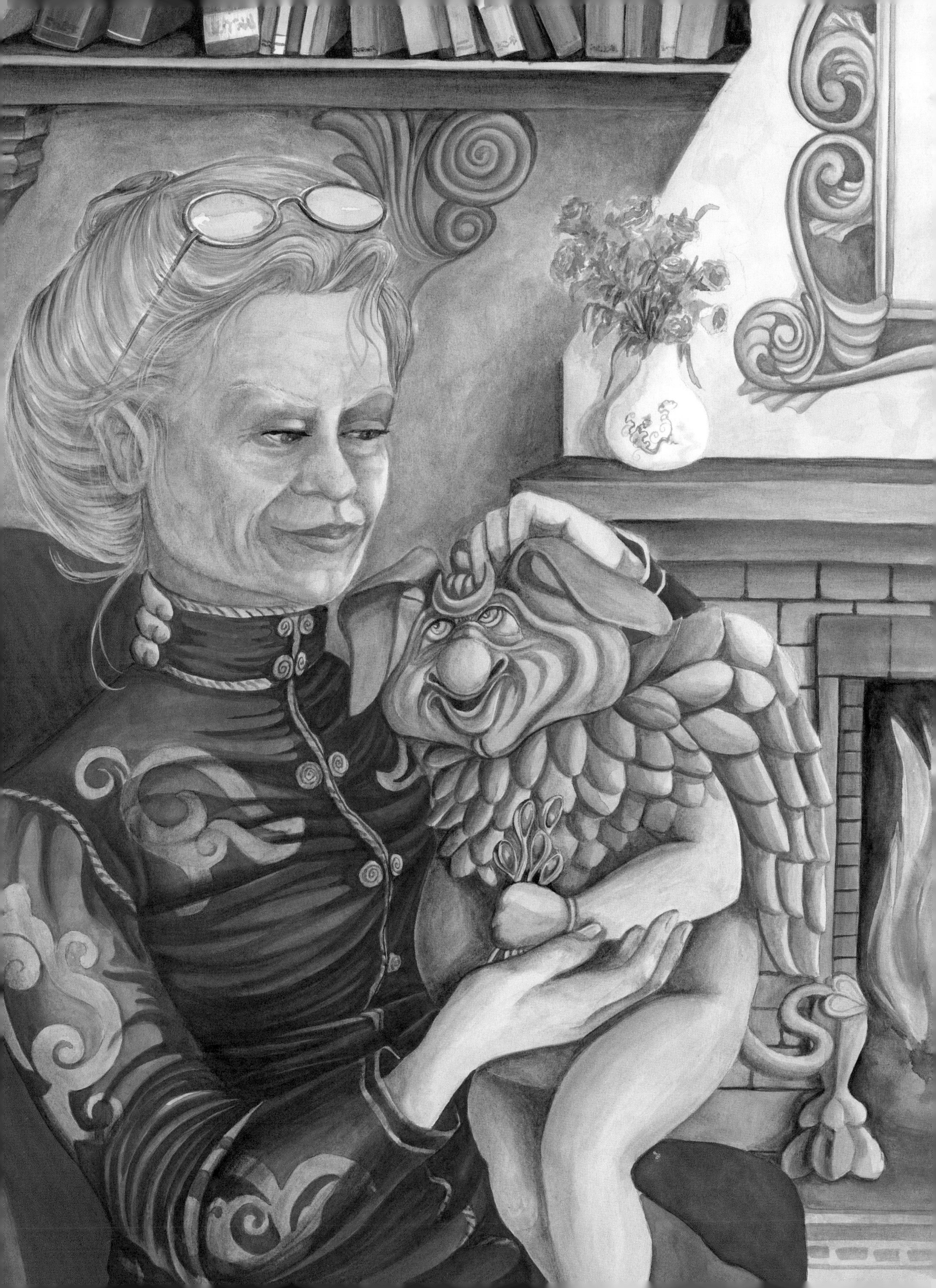

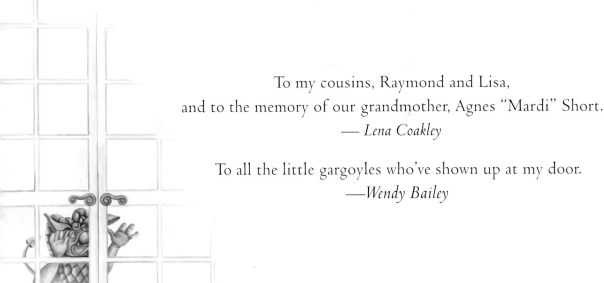

To my cousins, Raymond and Lisa,
and to the memory of our grandmother, Agnes "Mardi" Short.
— *Lena Coakley*

To all the little gargoyles who've shown up at my door.
—*Wendy Bailey*

National Library of Canada Cataloguing in Publication Data:

Coakley, Lena, 1967-
Mrs. Goodhearth and the gargoyle / Lena Coakley; Wendy Bailey, illustrator.

ISBN 1-55143-328-1

I. Bailey, Wendy II. Title.
PS8605.O234M58 2005   jC813'.6   C2005-902686-3

First published in the United States 2005

Library of Congress Control Number: 2005926378

Summary: A lonely gargoyle has a chance for friendship when an elderly woman moves into his house.

Orca Book Publishers gratefully acknowledges the support for its publishing programs
provided by the following agencies: the Government of Canada through the
Book Publishing Industry Development Program (BPIDP),
the Canada Council for the Arts, and the British Columbia Arts Council.

Typesetting and design by Lynn O'Rourke
Artwork created in acrylics
Scanning by Island Graphics, Victoria, BC

Orca Book Publishers
Box 5626 Stn. B
Victoria, BC Canada
V8R 6S4

Orca Book Publishers
PO Box 468
Custer, WA   USA
98240-0468

Printed and bound in Hong Kong
09 08 07 06 05 • 5 4 3 2 1